Fly the Unfriendly Skies

More **Strange Matter**™ from
Marty M. Engle & Johnny Ray Barnes, Jr.

Fly the Unfriendly Skies

Marty M. Engle

A MONTAGE PUBLICATION

Montage Publications, a Front Line company, San Diego, California

ISBN 1-56714-042-4

Printed in the U.S.A.

TO JON AND ALEX

My last life ended with a violent jerk in the coach class cabin of Flight 341. A sudden heart-stopping drop, a flash of lightning, a surge of terror, and it was all over.

I didn't have time to cry out or even whimper. I felt my heart freeze as I saw my sister Kelly's reflection in the glass.

How unfair. How could it be over? My fingers gripped the plastic case tightly. My arms tensed and locked in place. I closed my eyes in disbelief.

"Stupid plane. Lousy storm," I grumbled.

The screen flashed over and over: GAME OVER. GAME OVER. Life three ended with a careless plunge.

My sister punctuated my defeat in the usual manner. "HA! HA! Dead again. Give it up,

Morgan. Try another million times, but you'll NEVER beat my score."

"BULL! Only because of this stupid plane. I would have had you that time," I countered, turning the Game Boy off.

Another minute of staring at a green screen and I would throw up. Normally, I could kick her butt at *any* video game, but up here I couldn't concentrate.

I *hated* flying and the storm didn't help.

My name is Morgan Taylor and I'm twelve years old. I go to Fairfield Junior High with my evil sister, Kelly. Okay, she isn't evil, but she's a real pain sometimes. She has to be in the middle of everything and be the best one at it. The worst combination, athletic *and* pretty. She's in track and basketball and debate and on and on and on . . .

On the popularity scale, she's about an eight and I'm a lowly two. She has the best clothes and the best hair and a million friends.

I have *two* friends, Curtis Chatman and Darren Donaldson, and neither were on the plane with me when I could have used them.

Curt is the calmest guy I know. *Nothing* gets to him. Darren, on the other hand, is a spastic little bag of pent-up aggression . . . but he sure has a way of relieving a tense situation. We co-own a comic collection, even though he keeps it in *his* closet (for safer keeping, he says).

Lightning flashed outside the small, round window beside me. The plane rocked and shook. My fingers dug into the armrests, nudging Kelly's arm aside.

"HEY! I'm sitting here, too, you know. Stay in your own seat, all right?"

"Something's wrong. I can feel it."

My head pounded, and my stomach tied itself into a permanent knot. I kept seeing myself falling through the bottom of the plane, twisting and turning, the screams of the passengers echoing behind me.

Suddenly, the plane jerked and shook.

My heart squeezed in my chest. My forehead grew clammy with cold sweat. I knocked her arm off again, claiming the life-preserving armrests as my own.

"Move your arms! I'm dying here!"

"Grow *up*, Morgan. It's just a storm. We're not the *first* to fly in a storm. You're worrying over nothing. Lose another game or something . . . or do you need a pacifier?"

"Sorry. If something goes wrong, I don't

have a *broomstick* to fly off on, like you do." I would have smiled at my brilliant, biting remark, but another large bump put a grimace on my face instead.

"Oh, man. I need air," I stammered, reaching above me and turning the little air jet on high. "Let this end! PLEASE!"

"You're really scared, aren't you?" Kelly asked, wearing a half-concerned expression.

Another jolt knocked the words right out of me before I could stop them.

"WELL, DUH! I'M TERRIFIED, ALL RIGHT? WE ARE GOING TO DIE!" The sudden burst rang through the cabin, gathering attention as it went.

Everyone on the plane stared at us, from the attendants to the babies. All eyes locked on to the scaredy-cat in seat 23F.

They wouldn't stop staring.

An attendant started toward us.

"Oh, great."

"Brilliant, Morgan." Kelly popped a wad of gum in her big mouth, the same bright pink as her tank top.

The attendant leaned in, a Colgate smile covering her face. "Are you okay, young man?

Would you like a magazine or some more peanuts?"

"I would *like* to be on the ground, in our car and *away* from this crummy airplane." I clenched my fists and closed my eyes as another jolt rocked the plane.

Kelly leaned over. "Do you have something to render him unconscious for the rest of the trip?"

"We'll be on the ground very soon," the stewardess sighed, rolling her eyes and continuing toward the back.

"Quit worrying! Dad is probably already at the airport waiting to meet us," Kelly mumbled, picking through the magazines in the pouch in front of her.

"Don't worry, kid. It will all be over soon," the heavy man across from us laughed, still blasting away on his laptop computer. On the screen (in letters as red as his tie) . . . **D O O M!**

I have that game at home, on my Mac Performa. I played it every night for a month, until Mom caught me blasting away at two in the morning. Now I'm not supposed to play it at all.

Mom thinks I spend way too much time on the computer. She thinks I'm breaking into the Pentagon, or becoming the target of international spies, or bringing down the phone companies. Nothing that glamorous, I'm afraid.

Usually I'm on the Internet in the World Wide Web or the Usenet groups. Never as myself, of course. I have about twelve different names on-line, depending on the information I'm trying to get.

I even showed Dad how to buy our airline tickets from an on-line service!

The very tickets that put me on this deathtrap in the first place.

Hmmm. Maybe I *do* spend too much time on the computer.

A violent jerk rocked the cabin, dropping my heart into my stomach.

I pulled Kelly close. "I'm serious, Kelly. Something's wrong. I can feel it. Something is going to happen. Something bad."

The look on my face must have gotten to her. She said the words, even though I could tell she didn't believe them.

"It's just your imagination."

Suddenly, a scream filled the cabin, bringing my worst fears to life.

"OVER THERE! LOOK!" The voice boomed three rows ahead. A horrified young woman pointed to the window, sprang from her seat, and fell into the aisle. The college-aged kids sharing her row pressed their faces flat to the window.

"LOOK AT THAT!" one exclaimed.

"I'VE NEVER SEEN ANYTHING LIKE IT!" the other shouted.

I watched as the other side of the plane emptied and my side filled, the passengers from the opposite row of seats spilling into the aisles, craning their necks, anxious to see the source of excitement.

My first reaction: *look out the window!* Then I had second thoughts. Do I really want to know? What if an engine had caught fire? What

7

if the bolts holding the wing on were popping off, one by one? Could I stand it? Did I *really* want to know? My head swam with fatal possibilities and my breath quickened.

"What now?" Kelly huffed, thrusting her head to the window, popping a bubble loudly as she passed.

The gum fell out of her slack-jawed mouth and onto my lap.

"No way. . ."

The captain's voice crackled over the speaker with false confidence. "Ladies and gentlemen, I have to ask you to return to your seats and fasten your safety belts. An attendant will be by shortly to assist you."

I could hear the fear in his voice. My pulse started racing.

Look out the window! I yelled to myself.

I darted a glance to the window and saw the back of Kelly's head. She had climbed into my lap, shoving her whole head in the window. Several passengers crowded the aisle beside us.

"Move it, kid! Let us see!" They darted from side to side, as if that would make her move.

She wouldn't budge.

"Ladies and gentlemen, for safety's sake,

8

we ask you to please return to your se . . ." The captain cut himself off.

The attendants hurried down the aisle, arguing with passengers and forcing people back to the opposite rows.

"Kelly, let me see," I whispered softly.

No response.

"KELLY, let me see," I said again.

No response.

No one moved. Everyone stayed glued to the windows. The attendants joined the crowds, their heads crammed into the tiny windows as well.

I wiped the cold sweat from my forehead as I felt my face flush. I had to know. My mind raced with a thousand things that could be wrong outside.

I grabbed Kelly by her pink tank top and pulled her away from the window. She moved away effortlessly, as if in a trance.

I saw it.

A few hundred yards past the blinking green lights on the tip of the wing, a thin metal disk skipped and jerked through the night air, keeping pace with the plane.

It looked to be about half the size of the passenger section, black and silver plates placed lip to lip, a ring of blue lights circling the middle, blinking on and off in regular intervals. Three red lights circled past the blue lights in the opposite direction.

No exhaust. No wings. No fins.

A low black dome sat on top, cutting through the dark clouds.

"It's a UFO. *A real UFO!*" I said with astonishment, to no one in particular.

3

Everyone in the plane shouted and yelled at once, wondering what it could be.

"It's changing!" someone shouted.

"He's right! Look!" another agreed.

I found *myself* glued to the window, my face pressed to the glass. Kelly pulled and tugged at me, begging for another look.

It was changing!

An energy field surrounded it, causing the bottom of the disk to light up a blinding white-blue. The sides of the saucer warped, then ballooned and stretched, like I was looking at it through a spinning glass bottle. Clouds whirled over its surface as they passed, like cotton candy in a spinner.

My breath grew fast and short. Next to computers, UFOs were my favorite hobby! I had read everything possible about them; studied the pictures, watched the videos, but I never thought I'd see one.

A real UFO! hovering two hundred yards from me . . .

And something had to be flying it.

Day faded into night outside, and all I could see were the rings of lights and the steady green flash on the wing of the plane. I couldn't take my eyes off it. No one could.

"I hope someone's taping this!" a woman shouted. I noticed a stunned older man hold a video camera up in fast reply.

"LET ME SEE!" Kelly shouted and pulled me back, impatiently.

"WAIT! THERE'S ANOTHER!" Kelly screamed, pointing above the first.

I saw it then, too.

A dark object glided through the churning clouds like a shark, larger and shaped more like a boomerang than a saucer.

A giant flying boomerang descended, as black as the sky around it, easily keeping pace with the saucer and our plane.

Three bright-white lights, set in a triangular pattern, sprang to life on the bottom. They rotated around like spotlights, searching and turning, cutting through the clouds.

One light swept across the plane.

The cabin lit up as bright as daylight, sending everyone screaming and jerking away from the windows.

Everyone but me.

Terror paralyzed me as I watched the boomerang rotate over the saucer, about a hundred yards from the plane.

Another light swept down across the surface of the disk.

Discovered.

The other two beams from the boomerang craft locked on to the disk, matching its speed as it raced along with the plane.

The disk lurched to the side and flew under us fast. I saw only a blue-white streak vanish from sight, below the wing.

"It ran from that other ship! The boomerang-shaped one!" I yelled.

A blinding stream of green lightning shot out of the boomerang, streaking toward the disk ... *brushing the wing of the plane.*

A shower of metal and fire erupted from the wing as the stream sailed past.

Screams filled the cabin as people slammed into the floor, the plane rolling to the side, shaking violently.

"Ladies and gentlemen, we may experience some turbulence, please do not be alarmed," the captain announced as calmly as possible.

My stomach knotted and I found myself yelling, blinded with panic. I felt the strain of my safety belt as the plane continued to bounce and shake. Kelly fell to the floor and held onto her seat, sobbing uncontrollably.

The plane banked left, then straightened as dozens of frantic passengers hurried down the aisles, back to their seats.

Kelly struggled to her seat and fastened her belt. Her hand grabbed mine in desperation and squeezed, tears streaming down her cheeks.

Light flooded the cabin as I forced myself to look slowly to the right.

My chest tightened. My heart pounded. I tried to look away but couldn't.

I looked past my terrified sister and past the people scrambling down the aisle.

The saucer slowly rose up and *filled* the window in the row across from me. It hovered *inches* off the wing.

It looked like a giant Peeping Tom, leering in the windows at the terrified passengers.

A ball of green lightning suddenly gathered on the rim of the disk and . . . *fired.*

Right for the cabin!

They stopped the plane.

The disk grabbed the plane with a lasso of green lightning and held it in midair.

The impact of the sudden stop hit like a bomb. Carry-on bags, food trays, magazines, and laptop computers all flew through the air like missiles and slammed into the walls and seats.

"KELLY! Are you okay? KELLY?"

"MORGAN! BEHIND YOU!" Kelly pointed, her eyes large and frightened.

I glanced out the window and saw the boomerang craft descend, turn and hover a few feet from the left wing.

I looked across the aisle and saw the saucer out the other window, or I should say, windows. It ran at least twenty windows in length, staying mere inches from the wing.

The whole plane started to glow the same weird blue glow as the saucer's underside.

'T-They stopped us, Kelly. We aren't moving," I stammered.

Boxed in. The boomerang craft on the left side. The saucer on the right.

"This is the captain speaking. I am asking all of you to remain seated, your seat belt securely fastened, and stay calm. We are in contact with the tower, trying to . . . assess our situation."

The speaker shorted out.

Along with all the lights, the air conditioning, the radios, and the portable computers.

Panic filled the cabin as people scrambled into their seats. The air filled with sobs and cries as the last of the seat belts clicked shut.

The man across from us had lost his laptop in the sudden stop. His big chest heaved with each sob, his eyes squinched tightly shut.

The cabin filled with the steady flash of red, blue, and white lights from the alien crafts outside.

The oxygen masks dropped from the overhead compartments like unfurling coils.

I didn't see the attendants anywhere! I needed assistance, and needed it badly! I grabbed the cup and shakily pulled it over my nose.

I wondered if the cockpit controls had shorted out, too. Not that it mattered. The saucer had us trapped, the only thing keeping us in the air.

I checked my seat belt again as Kelly clenched my hand tighter.

I thought of how it must look to the people in the control tower. A screen must have told them that Flight 341 to Fairfield had stopped in midair.

Suddenly, the cabin turned deathly quiet.

All attention turned to the very front of the plane.

I couldn't see over the seat in front of me, but I saw the flare and heard a lady scream!

A yellow flash exploded down the aisle, and something up near the cockpit sounded like it blew open.

I heard people shouting from the front of the plane, but no one seemed to be budging from their seats.

Shouts and muffled screams spread from row to row, front to back, closer and closer as I noticed a strange yellow mist spreading thinly across the floor.

An odd light-headedness came over me. I felt woozy, panicky. Things began to look unreal, fuzzy, like in a dream. I felt drugged.

It had to be the yellow mist.

The screams and shouts drew closer.

Something was working its way down the aisle, row by row.

A mixed sense of dread and wonder flooded my mind. What would an extraterrestrial look like? Would it be human, or some hideous monster, like in *It Came From Another World*.

What did they want? Why *this* plane?

Kelly turned to me, her head swaying and bouncing. I could tell the mist had affected her, too. Were the rest of the passengers drugged, like us? I could barely hear her over the yelling and shouting.

"What is it, Morgan? What's going on?"

"I think something's coming down the aisle. We've been boarded. S-S-Stay quiet," I stammered.

"NO WAY! We have to get out of here!"

Kelly unbuckled her seat belt with shaking hands and carefully stood up, almost losing her balance, peering down the aisle.

"Kelly, noooo! Sit dooown," I slurred. Where did she plan on going? We were thirty thousand feet in the air!

She slowly peeked over the top of the seat and promptly screamed.

My head spun, my senses deadened. "KELLY!" I shouted, unbuckling my seat belt.

Too late.

Her scream stopped when a pale grey hand clamped over her mouth and eased her slowly back into her seat.

A figure about four feet tall stood in the aisle and leaned in toward us. Light grey skin stretched tightly over his skeletal frame. Huge black eyes stared unblinking from his oversized head. His tiny nose twitched over a simple slit-like mouth, opening and closing very slightly.

Like a dream, but undoubtedly real. I couldn't take my eyes off him.

He blinked at me.

Two more figures appeared behind him as the light yellow mist drifted up from the floor.

With one hand on Kelly's mouth, he pulled a small silver cylinder out of a pocket in his jumpsuit. I had thought they weren't wearing any clothes at first, but now I noticed they all wore jumpsuits made of a material so tight and thin, it fit them like a second skin.

He ran the cylinder over her wrist and looked at a small window on top.

His eyes widened and looked upset, agitated, almost sad. *What did it tell him?*

With a fast nod to his friends, he grabbed Kelly and pulled her into the aisle. She kicked and screamed with all the power her drugged-up thirteen-year-old body could muster.

"HEY! LET HER GO!"

My head cleared slightly, stirred by the sight of my frantically struggling sister. I unsteadily shot out of my seat. I'm not a very good fighter, but I sure couldn't sit by and let them take my sister.

I tackled the one holding Kelly. His eyes grew even wider and I could have sworn he looked surprised! The drug made it hard to move my arms and legs, as if I was wading through mud.

Kelly accidentally kicked me square in the chin. "OWWW!"

"HELP ME! MORGAN, HELP!" Kelly whimpered, yanking and struggling at the wiry grey limbs that held her. No use. The drug had sapped her strength, too.

An other being grabbed me, picked me up and ran down the aisle toward the front of the plane.

The other passengers all seemed to be on the verge of unconsciousness, even the ones with oxygen masks on. Their heads moved from side to side with moans and frightened cries, but they couldn't stand up or fight. The yellow mist drifted across them.

Dozens of little grey aliens moved from passenger to passenger, checking a select few with the silver cylinders. I noticed one man wince when they pressed the silver and black tip to his wrist. It sounded like an air gun as they pulled it away.

One group of aliens peered anxiously out the windows, staring at the boomerang craft, chattering nervously and hurrying the others along. They seemed to be watching for someone or *something* from the *other* craft.

They carried hand-held, box-like devices coiled to small packs on their belts, and crouched down behind seats and in the aisles, as if expecting an army to come through the back of the plane.

Weapons, I thought as we reached the front of the plane. *Who's in the other craft?*

The alien kept pulling me along, so I didn't have time to study the devices.

No sound stirred from the cockpit as we passed, the yellow mist drifting under the jamb.

An attendant was curled into the corner near the front lavatory, sobbing and screaming in hysterical bursts, as two grey aliens examined her with a silver cylinder.

A flash of lightning outlined the *opened* airplane door!

I couldn't believe it! The door was open at 30,000 feet! No vacuum, no rush of air, no loud roar. How? The stormy clouds churned in the dead blue-black sky, open to the plane.

Suddenly my heart froze in terror.

The grey alien held me tightly, ran to the door and jumped out.

I looked straight down at the black void that led to the ground, miles and miles below. The grey alien released his grip as we tumbled, end over end.

A shrill screech wheezed from my throat as I felt the *nothing* around me.

He killed me.

An alien from another world *killed* me. *He threw me from a plane!*

I noticed the bottoms of Kelly's expensive sneakers and realized the grey alien who held her had jumped too!

But wait. How could I be screaming? I shouldn't have even been able to draw a breath, let alone scream. I felt no rush of wind. No sensation of falling.

Then I saw the yellow rings of light

passing me, one after another.

A tube. A twisty, turning tube of light was pulling us under the belly of the plane, across the wing and into a hatch on the top of the saucer. It sealed off the door of the plane and served as an umbilical cord to the huge flying disk.

My head spun, my eyes throbbed from behind. I felt a wave of nausea and a strange dull pain behind my nose. My eyes drifted closed.

I forced them back open.

I saw the black hatch on top of the saucer drawing closer, just over the seam where the two plates come together, over the spinning rings of red and blue lights.

A high, shrill whistle sounded in my ears, and my nose started to bleed. I would pass out in a moment. I could feel my eyes closing again.

The grey alien that jumped with me turned himself to face me, his shiny black eyes shielded by a thick, white membrane. He held a thin, bony finger to his mouth . . .

and smiled.

My eyes drifted open lazily, half-drugged. I found myself in a chair, a wheelchair I guessed, being pushed down a long, curving corridor.

Rectangular lights ran along the wall, above the windows, spaced inches apart. Millions of stars shone through the windows against the blackest sky I had ever seen. Darker than the sky from the plane.

I turned my head slowly and saw Kelly in a similar chair, being pushed along beside me. Her head flopped to the side as her eyes fluttered. The wall, made of bright white metal panels, passed slowly beside her.

For a moment I couldn't remember anything. Had the plane crashed? Was I in a hospital? My head felt taped together. My arms and legs felt as heavy as lead.

A strange device, shaped like a dentist's drill, craned in over Kelly's head, a bright light shining from the tip.

"Kelly. L . . . Look out." I could barely speak. The words slurred. No use. Her head spilled forward, as groggy as mine. The chairs continued moving slowly ahead.

Suddenly her head snapped back as the light pressed flatly to her forehead. She moaned as another light pushed into her wrists, piercing the skin.

"No. Stop. What are you doing to her?" I wanted to protest, to stop the mechanical arms, but I felt too weak to move.

The light tips pulsed erratically from yellow to white with a strange clicking sound.

As suddenly as they had sprung up, the devices craned away and retracted into the chair.

"Kelly? Are you all right?"

No answer. Only a moan.

An odd, yet familiar, smell made me wince. *Antiseptic.* We had to be in a hospital.

I heard a strange voice, high-pitched and chattering like a chipmunk's, crackling over a speaker. Terrible sound system. Worse than a drive-through speaker at a fast-food place. Only

I couldn't see any speakers anywhere.

I couldn't see any *doors* anywhere, either. Occasionally, a hallway would intersect with ours, like a spoke on a wheel.

I thought I saw one of the panels slide open behind me, two nurses or something walking out, but I couldn't be sure.

Then I noticed the Earth coming into view outside the window.

The Earth!

I yelled and leaped from the chair.

I stumbled and caught myself, a jolting shock of terror racing through my body. My mind cleared rapidly, filling with disbelief.

Behind me, two grey aliens held the handles to the boxy, floating chairs. They looked as shocked as I did.

I grabbed Kelly by the hand and pulled her from the chair, shouting hysterically. She tumbled to the floor as the aliens backed cautiously away.

"C'MON! KELLY! C'MON!" I cried out, yanking her to her feet.

Kelly woozily turned and saw the grey aliens, running in the opposite direction, pushing the chairs as fast they could. The shock pulled her out of her daze as she regained her footing.

"Those were . . . th . . . they're . . .," Kelly stammered.

"Aliens!" I replied, backing away.

"Then we're in . . ."

"Space! RUN! RUN FOR IT!"

A high-pitch beep sounded down the hall, loud and steady, repeating in short bursts.

Our feet pounded against the soft, padded floor. My sense of balance returned slowly as the drug wore off. My eyes darted everywhere, but always came back to the Earth hanging like a big, blue marble outside the windows.

"Where are we going? What are we going to do?" Kelly shrieked. The sight of the Earth hanging in the window stopped her, practically knocking her off her feet.

"COME ON!" I yelled, tugging her along. "WE HAVE TO HIDE!"

"HIDE?! WHERE?" Kelly screeched, following me into a side corridor.

"BE QUIET! They'll find us!"

I had seen one of the panels slide open before. I knew it. Now I had to figure out how to make it work for me.

I picked a panel toward the middle of the hall and started feeling around the edges.

"HURRY!" Kelly yelled.

The speaker system crackled to life again, a distressed chattering filling my ears along with the high-pitched beep, probably an alarm of some sort.

"Forget it! Let's try another one," Kelly said breathlessly.

A small group of shadows hit the floor at the end of the hall and drew closer, mingling together, then apart. They were coming.

A box-like device emerged from around the corner, a grey hand clutching it.

"MORGAN! HURRY!"

I noticed a small extrusion halfway up the panel, like a square covering with an open end. Hand-sized. Perfect.

"Stick your hand in there, quick!" I whispered.

"Are you nuts? YOU DO IT!" Her eyes grew wide as a grey head began to cautiously peek around the corner.

"Great."

I shoved my hand in and felt a slight tingle as a bright light flashed.

The panel slid open.

We hurried in, ducking our heads, and the panel closed behind us with a sigh.

The room was as large as my bedroom closet, and about as comfortable. We crouched down among small metal crates, which were stacked to the ceiling. They had rounded corners and a strange latch attached to a small window, like a display screen.

"They saw us. I know they did!" Kelly hit me hard on the shoulder. "We can't stay here! What are we going to do?"

"I don't know, all right? Do you know how to fly a UFO?"

"TALK TO THEM! Make them take us back. You read all that science fiction junk all the time! *Say* something to them."

"Get a clue! This is *reality*. I don't speak little grey alien! We don't know what they want or what they'll do!"

A click sounded from the panel which had closed behind us. A small bank of lights started blinking on the wall next to it.

"Through there!" I whispered, pointing to a narrow opening in the back wall, just above the floor. It seemed to be a vent or something, uncovered and just big enough to crawl through.

I could feel the air blowing through as I wiggled in.

"Come on!"

Kelly crouched against the crates, shaking her head.

"Come on, NOW!"

The panel began to slide open.

Kelly shoved me along as she crawled through the opening, a beam of light striking the floor where she had been a moment before, searching around erratically.

"This way," I whispered.

A pale red light flashed on and off about thirty feet away, around a sharp turn in the shaft.

We started crawling.

"Where are we going?" Kelly asked.

"I don't know. Away from them. It won't take them long to figure out where we went. I need to find a place to stop and think."

"About . . ."

"About what to do."

"What to do? I'll *tell* you what we're going to do. We're going to find the captain or the

34

president or the leader or whatever they call the thing in charge here and tell *it* to take us home!"

"Hello? Grow a brain, please. Did you notice anyone *else* from the plane on board this ship?"

"No."

"Well, they didn't take *us* on board for a sightseeing trip, that's for sure."

"Just because we haven't seen anyone else from the plane yet doesn't mean they're not here," she huffed. Her breathing sounded raspy, heavy. Too heavy.

"Didn't you see what they did to you on the plane? Small, grey, and ugly checked you over with this metal tube thing, and he didn't seem too thrilled about what it told him."

She stopped crawling.

"What?"

"Look, they only checked a few people like they checked you. And they gave *them* shots or something."

"What do you mean?" she asked, a shiver in her voice.

"I mean *you* have to be something special. They didn't give you a shot. They took you on-board instead."

"Why?"

In my mind I watched the robot arms with strange lights attach to her forehead and wrists. I remembered the clicking and blinking. I stopped crawling and looked back over my shoulder. I didn't want to scare her any more than she was already.

"I don't know."

"Why'd they take *you*, then?"

"I don't know," I grumbled quietly as I crawled around a corner of the shaft. "Maybe because I came after you."

A red light flashed from the outside of a grate covering the end of the shaft.

The grate led to a room full of small lights. I could see them flashing and blinking through the gloom.

"What is it?"

"It's another room. I'm going closer."

"Not alone, you're not."

The temperature climbed about thirty degrees in the last ten feet of the shaft. A thin, hot stream of air poured through the grate and across my hands.

I eased up to the grate and looked in.

9

A large tower, dotted with rectangular lights, stretched up to a domed ceiling at least fifty feet high.

Three rows of consoles, about two feet high, circled the base of the tower.

Dozens of little grey aliens sat in front of the consoles on stools that came out of the floor. Not separate pieces of furniture, but part of the floor and way too low for a human being to sit on comfortably.

Control panels, I supposed.

Three levels of metal catwalks ran from the tower to various corridors.

The room itself glowed under the bright red lights set in a circular pattern in the domed ceiling.

Small crates partially covered the opening

of the shaft and even more had been stacked in a rough semi-circle around it, creating a little wall . . .

And the perfect hiding place.

We would be safe there, at least for the time being.

A group of aliens gathered near the tower, their boxy weapons drawn. They chattered like crazy, waving their arms, extremely upset.

"What do you see?" Kelly whispered from behind me.

"You don't want to know."

"I can't stay in here much longer."

I looked back and noticed Kelly's flushed face and splotchy skin. Her arms trembled and she looked like she could pass out at any moment.

In my mind, I saw those robot arms attach to her forehead and wrists again; the lights pulsating, and the weird clicking sound.

"What did they do to you?" I whispered.

"What?" she rasped.

"Nothing. Okay. Let's get out of here . . . but stay low."

I eased the grate off with no problem and crept to the floor, about three feet below, slinking behind the crates.

Kelly followed.

The red light over the grate whirled.

I finally slumped to the floor with my back to the crates and tried to calm down. As long as we stayed low, they couldn't see us.

My heart throbbed in my chest. Wave after wave of nervous panic traveled up my spine. I felt like a trapped animal.

No way the saucer I saw from the plane could have been this big. No way!

They took us to a mother ship when we passed out.

They took us into orbit.

ORBIT!

No rescue. No Army fighters. No rescue helicopters. No space shuttle happening by. Nothing.

Helpless.

Hopeless.

Sheer, blind desperation created some ridiculous solutions in my head. I found myself whispering out loud to keep my sanity.

"Okay. We're trapped on an alien ship. There's two of us and about a hundred of them. We *take control of the ship!* Wait! For all we know *this* is the control room. There's no way we could fly this thing! That's just bunk you see in the movies. You know? Well, this is *reality!* Right, Kelly? That leaves us with two options."

"Morgan."

"I'm thinking, Kelly. Number one, we could give ourselves up and beg to be returned home."

"Morgan."

"Just a minute, Kelly. Of course, that assumes they can understand English, which they probably don't. Two. We can give ourselves up and . . . *see what happens.* Oh, man, that option *stinks!*"

"Morgan, I feel terrible."

I looked over to Kelly and nearly lost it. Her eyes looked like black glass marbles. Her face sagged like a wet sack. She propped herself against a crate opposite me, her trembling arms barely supporting her body.

I wanted to crawl over to her but couldn't make myself.

She was horribly sick.

The aliens must have given her some sort of illness. *Was I next?* Is that what they were injecting those people with? Did the robot arms put something in her body?

"What did they do to you, Kelly?" I felt tears pool in my eyes. My breathing shallowed as I crawled over to my sister.

"Morgan, I feel like I'm going to throw up." She coughed and wheezed.

"Don't. Try to be quiet. They'll find us."

"I'm freezing."

Impossible. It had to be at least a hundred degrees in there. Her skin took on a bluish cast. Her lips trembled.

"Oh, man. Kelly. I don't know what to do!" I started crying. Tears rolled down my face, no matter how hard I tried to keep them back.

Kelly could be dying, and there was nothing I could do.

Suddenly, the crates stacked around us slid to the floor. A dozen sinister black eyes glared at us behind pointed weapons.

The aliens found us.

"NO! Stay back!" I cried as the grey aliens pushed closer, their weapons drawn.

Kelly slid to the floor, too weak to move, and barely conscious.

I ran in front of her, thrusting my hands out in protest. "I mean it! I don't know what you did to her, but BACK OFF!"

I heard a strange, wet noise behind me.

Maybe if I had turned, I would have seen Kelly convulsing, unable to breathe.

The aliens pushed closer, cautiously.

"STOP! DON'T TOUCH US! I want to talk to the thing in charge! Who's in CHARGE here! ANSWER ME!"

If I had turned, maybe I would have seen her changing, melting, folding in on herself. I would have seen the steady rush of water coming from her ears, nose and eyes.

The aliens stopped moving. They froze like statues, their eyes wide and full of fear.

The weapons dropped from their hands like useless toys.

"What? What is it?" I asked.

They began to back away, slowly, staring at something behind me.

I turned to see it, far too late.

11

It hovered directly in front of me.

The name escaped my mouth, although I knew it wouldn't respond.

"Kelly?"

My heart jolted, my legs weakened and I felt like throwing up.

The tips of her fingers dissolved, the last recognizable piece of her.

In place of my sister hovered *a perfect sphere of black, rippling water.*

It floated in midair, about a foot off the ground, dripping steadily onto the floor.

It sounded like a fountain, with a faint, angry voice hidden inside. The surface rippled and criss-crossed, like a penny tossed in a pond. It shook and rolled in on itself angrily.

I backed slowly away, the aliens behind

me. We all crept backward together, never taking our eyes off the Kelly-thing.

They seemed as scared as I.

I turned my head to the side carefully, not looking away from the shaking, angry Kelly-thing. A waterblob.

"My sister?"

The alien next to me nodded. Even if he didn't understand English, he knew what I meant.

My sister was no longer human.

The black waterblob rose high in the air, swelling and contracting, like an animal breathing. It roared like a waterfall, the voice hidden inside shouting with anger in words I couldn't understand.

It spilled from itself, pouring from the bottom, splashing the floor and the toppled crates. The grey aliens screeched loudly and ran, scattering in all directions.

"WAIT! WHAT IS THAT THING? WHAT DO I DO?" I shouted.

It stopped. I had gotten its attention.

It raced down toward me, a hurricane set in a sphere three feet wide.

My hands flew up to stop it, my legs frozen in fear. A gasp swelled in my throat as I braced for impact.

A grey hand grabbed my shoulder and yanked me to the side.

The waterblob hit the floor with the force of a meteor, exactly where I stood only a moment before.

It erupted into a wide black pool, bubbled, then reformed into a stormy sphere.

The alien who had pulled me to the side grabbed my hand, startling me. He nodded his head quickly to the side, signalling me to follow him.

What other choice did I have?

We ran down a narrow aisle between the consoles, racing up to the tower in the center of the room.

The sound of screeching aliens, exploding control panels and a high, piercing buzz filled my head.

The alien pulled me along, right up to the tower, in front of a small hand pad.

Glancing around, I noticed small doors spaced evenly on the walls around the perimeter of the room.

"EXITS! LET'S GO!"

The alien stopped me, grabbing my shoulder, shaking his head frantically.

The doors had already started to slowly slide shut, dozens of grey aliens scrambling through just in time.

The alien who saved me touched the hand pad on the tower. Then he touched it again, impatiently, staring up at the top of the tower.

I looked around nervously, searching for the waterblob, but saw only the network of catwalks towering overhead, leading to the exits on three higher levels. The catwalks intersected the tower like spokes on a bicycle wheel.

The waterblob had vanished . . . but to where?

Smoke wafted up through the mesh steel flooring. "Where did it go? What did you things do to my sister!"

I started to grab the alien to get his full attention, but stopped when I heard the rushing sound of water.

Suddenly, the grey alien screeched, grabbed me, and jumped to the side, barely dodging the waterblob as it flooded past us in a thundering wave.

"I didn't even see it!" I screamed, ducking my head as the alien's large black eyes tracked the creature.

Pencil thin beams of green light sprang from a boxy weapon he yanked from his jumpsuit.

"NO! YOU'LL HURT HER!" I cried, knocking the box from his hands.

The beams arced wildly through the air, bouncing off the waterblob's surface into a catwalk above, slicing it in two with a shower of sparks.

The waterblob screamed in pain!

For a moment, it broke apart into smaller bobbing spheres, but rejoined itself quickly.

The alien turned desperately from the stunned waterblob and slammed the tower's hand pad with both hands.

In reluctant response, a panel of lights blinked on . . . *two levels above.*

An elevator. It had to be an elevator, but it was on the third level!

"She's gonna *kill us!* We have to get out of here, NOW!"

The alien scowled at me.

The waterblob drifted to a stop about twenty feet away. The waves of oily water on its surface churned and splashed, whipping into a storm.

My alien friend's chest rose and fell

rapidly. He pressed himself tightly against the wall of the tower, his eyes wide in fear.

The moment we leaned in either direction, the waterblob would slide to counter it . . . cornering its prey.

"What's happening to it?" I cried out as I watched the waterblob puff up, as if taking a deep breath.

The elevator hit the second level, passing the destroyed catwalk. Only one level to go.

My eyes darted back to the waterblob. It had swelled to five times its normal size!

"WHAT IS IT DOING?" I gasped.

Suddenly, the alien beside me screamed, like nails on a chalkboard!

The enormous waterblob caved in on itself at once, *spitting* a jet of water, like a cannon!

We ducked to the sides as it struck the tower, punching *a two foot hole* in the elevator door.

"NO!" I cried, as steam flooded my face.

The alien grabbed me, pulling me into the elevator, the smoldering hole sliding to the side as the door panel opened.

I fell against the back wall as the alien pressed a lit, flat pad next to the opening.

The door slid shut almost immediately, bringing the two foot hole in the door back with it.

My mouth dropped open, dread rising in my throat.

Through the hole I saw the ball of black water racing straight for me, charging the elevator.

"UP! UP NOW!" I screamed, kicking at the floor, as if I could back into the wall any further.

The alien quickly pressed the pad again. The light behind it died with a whine, as did the lights in the elevator. He struck it hard with his fist . . . nothing.

Through the hole, I saw only a wall of black water.

The alien sprang up to the ceiling of the elevator, pushing through an emergency trapdoor that folded to the side on contact.

In a flash, he vanished, scrambling up and out of the elevator car.

"HELP ME! PLEASE!" I yelled.

His long, grey arm thrust down through the opening, his hand extended.

I jumped.

A flood of black water poured through the hole in the door, flooding it like a pool, my legs kicking about a foot above it.

I looked down and saw the water below me, sloshing into the walls like tidal waves.

The alien pulled me up and through, slinging me to a narrow ledge that circled the elevator shaft. *I was inside the tower.*

He jumped to the ledge on the opposite side, kicking a small, flat pad on the side of the shaft.

The elevator immediately plunged out of sight, a flash of light trailing the walls with it as it slid away.

Far away.

The shaft seemed to go on forever, plunging into blackness.

I turned to the alien that saved my life, balanced on the ledge across from me.

"That was my sister." I felt tears swelling in my eyes. "She's gone."

The elevator shaft seemed to go on forever. We had been climbing the handles cut into the sides of the walls for at least fifteen minutes. My hands hurt and my legs grew weaker with every step.

Each step up became more tortured, more difficult. I knew I still had to think about myself ... but I kept feeling Kelly clutching my hand on the plane. I could see her terrified face in the chair and her sick, sad eyes when the aliens found us.

She picked on me a lot. She made me feel bad sometimes. Made me feel like a total nerd about my comic collection, about my sci-fi video collection, about my video games.

But ... she got in a fight with Kyle Banner once, when he knocked my lunch tray to the ground and wouldn't stop pushing me. No one else would help, but Kelly did.

Gone.

I missed her already.

"How much further?" I asked.

The grey alien didn't answer. He continued to climb like a spider; his long, thin limbs cycling in a climbing motion, his hands wrapping firmly around each handle.

I tried, as much as possible, not to look at him. I wanted to forget what he looked like and where he came from. The only thing I could count on, so far, was his help.

But why?

They changed Kelly. They must have. That cylinder did something when they passed it over her on the plane, or maybe the arms from that chair injected her with something. I couldn't be sure, but I knew they did it to her. They turned her into a monster; a monster that wanted to kill *me,* her own brother.

I continued to climb, dreading each handle, fear crawling down my straining back. For all I knew, he could be taking me to some other room to kill me, or cook me, or worse.

That didn't make any sense, though. He

could have just let that *thing* kill me.

Why spare me? Why help me?

I had the feeling I wouldn't get any answers from my new "friend".

A loud chattering erupted from his mouth. He pointed straight up, his black eyes narrowing.

Above us, about ten feet away, I saw the lit outline of a door in the wall of the shaft.

I swallowed hard. Could my doom be ten feet away?

"Why are you doing this? Why are you helping me?" I looked searchingly at the small, slit-like mouth, the narrow nose, the mirror-black eyes, searching for the slightest sign of an answer.

He simply pointed up again, and climbed faster, chattering loudly.

We pulled ourselves up onto the narrow ledge that circled the shaft, and rested beside the door. My chest heaved and I could hardly draw a breath.

I looked down the dark shaft below me.

Nothing there. I couldn't even see where we had started our climb.

I kept wishing Kelly could be beside me, to help me out of this mess. She could be bossy, picky, aggravating, and sometimes, even mean. To be honest, sometimes I could be just as bad to her. But when it really came down to it, we always did our best to help each other out.

That wasn't going to happen this time.

This time I was on my own.

"Open the door. Let's get this over with," I said, taking one last look down.

He fixed me with a glance and signalled me to the side, away from the door. He wanted me to stay out of sight.

"Why?"

He glared angrily, at least it looked like anger, and signalled again. I didn't argue.

He pressed the small white rectangle beside the door.

The panel slid open as he stepped through, into what sounded like a flurry of activity and chattering.

Light suddenly flashed through the door, along with horrid scratchy noises and loud, alien screeching.

The noises startled me, making me back away from the door, a sudden wave of panic sweept through me, pushing me to my breaking point!

For a moment, the full reality of my surroundings hit me. I felt totally helpless. Utterly alone. Tears swelled in my eyes. I tried in vain to understand the harsh alien screeching in the room beside me, desperate to make sense of something. Of anything! The unfamiliar sights, sounds, and smells, everything seemed absolutely foreign, unrecognizable.

I kept looking around the shaft, glancing toward the door, hoping that someone *human* would walk through, telling me that everything would be fine and that I could leave any time I wanted.

My eyes widened as the screeching stopped.

A long, grey hand poked around the corner of the door and the bony grey finger started curling, telling me to come in.

No one could help me now. Not Mom or Dad, or Kelly. No one. I had only myself to count on, and blind trust in something that wasn't even human.

I steadied my nerves and wiped my eyes, stepping to the opened door, red flashes of light bouncing on my face.

Dozens of grey aliens lowered their

57

weapons as I walked into a small control area, scared expressions twisting their thin faces, which followed my every move.

The walls of the room were lined with a thin mesh of metal bars, reminding me of a cage. A red spotlight swept across the floor, dimly lighting two low control consoles and two chairs that sat in front of a dark, thick glass wall.

The crowded room divided as I continued to walk forward.

My friend walked up to a control console and pressed a series of small pads.

Large, white spotlights switched on, echoing loudly, flooding a large round room behind the glass wall.

What I saw made me tremble in awe and terror. My eyes screamed to look away, my brain refusing to accept what lay before me.

In the room behind the glass wall, I saw hundreds and hundreds of icy, clear canisters, about three feet high . . . *each containing a frozen sphere of black water.*

Spheres of black water. Just like Kelly.
Victims.

"No," I choked, stepping forward.

The aliens exploded into a flurry of

activity as my friend placed his hand on my shoulder.

Startled, I turned to face him.

He grabbed my other shoulder and locked his gaze to mine.

His body became rigid, his black eyes turned a bright, glowing blue.

A shocking jolt surged through my body. I couldn't feel the floor beneath me or his hands on my shoulders. I tried to turn my head away but couldn't.

A white flash enveloped my mind and I could hear a faint static, like television noise, deep in my head.

14

I sat up with a startled gasp. My eyes blinked rapidly, darting all around, grasping for some clue as to where I was.

The familiar stripes of my wallpaper started to form from the dark, followed by my shelves and my videotapes with the all too familiar titles of *The Day the Earth Stood Still*, *Forbidden Planet*, and *Tron*.

The VCR under the TV whirred and clicked, still playing the tape I had forgotten to turn off, *John Carpenter's: THE THING*.

Overhead, a model of a super-secret spy plane, the Aurora Interceptor, swayed from its strings: a gift from my good friend Darren.

The tree outside my window swayed in a light breeze. The pale pink street light glowed behind it.

I breathed a sigh of relief and rubbed the back of my head.

A dream. I knew it had to be a dream.

No aliens. No saucers or boomerang craft. No big blobs of black water.

Kelly was still alive.

"ALIVE! Just like me!" I shouted, laughing outright and jumping out of bed. "What a relief!"

I took a moment to breathe. Everything smelled familiar; my room, my clothes, the air. From the hearty aroma of half-eaten pizza on my night stand, to the dusty, wooden scent of my desk. I welcomed them all.

Then I saw them.

The culprits responsible for my hideous experience peeked out from under my blanket, books like *Above Top Secret* and *Dimensions*. Beside my bed sat more stacks of books, different shapes and sizes, all on UFO's and alien abduction.

I picked up the VCR remote and pressed 'stop' just as MacReady prepared to test some guy's blood for alien infection in a small glass dish.

Maybe I *am* reading too much about this stuff.

"No way I can go back to sleep. Not now," I muttered, falling into the chair in front of my desk. "Let's see if you're through."

I had been downloading a computer file off the Internet before I went to bed.

As the monitor of my Mac Performa faded into light, I removed the sock that dangled across the top, tossed there in a quick bid to get to bed.

On the screen I noticed the file still had another hour to go, the bytes ticking down *painfully* slow. I needed a new modem, a faster modem. This one ran way too *slow!*

"It'll be worth it," I groaned, spinning around in my chair.

The file contained all kinds of compressed pictures of different UFO sightings from a book which had just been released. The guys who did the book put all their pictures up for grabs on the Internet in their own World Wide Web page.

The book sounded really good. It was all about the history of wrecked flying saucers. Like the one in Roswell, New Mexico, in 1947, where the Army supposedly found a crashed saucer in the desert with three dead aliens and one live one. The Army first reported it as a flying saucer, but then took it back, and said it was a weather balloon instead.

In interviews years later, everyone involved said it *was* a crashed saucer and that higher authorities made them make up a cover story because they didn't want anyone to know.

Come to think of it, the aliens they supposedly found looked a lot like the aliens in my dream, the grey ones.

The coolest part of the book is about a dry lake bed in Nevada known as Groom Lake and the top secret Air Force base located there.

They supposedly have nine flying saucers, in all different shapes and sizes, all in perfect condition.

They've also been rumored to have engineers from all over the country working on them. Some of them say the saucers are real alien ships, but others say they are made by the Air Force, kept secret from the public.

According to the book, a scientist who used to work there says that the saucers are powered by a metal known as element 115, a metal so dense it couldn't possibly form naturally on earth.

The metal is put into a reaction chamber

where it creates a field of energy that pushes the ship along.

Like the blue-white energy field that surrounded the saucer outside the plane in my dream.

Unfortunately the book really doesn't have an ending, just like the real mystery of UFO's. Could it all be a giant hoax or a *dream?*

"Ugh! Another half hour for that stupid file," I muttered, turning off the monitor.

I had the computer set to log off automatically after it was through downloading the file, so I didn't need to wait up. The red lights on the modem blinked steadily.

I strolled over to the window and looked up at the night sky. A million stars twinkled brightly with not a cloud in sight.

Tomorrow night, I would be right up there with them. Flying in a 737, nonstop to Greendale with Kelly.

I usually had fun on my summertime visits to my aunt, except I always dreaded the plane ride, tomorrow's flight being no exception.

I hated heights, and hated the feeling of falling even more.

Wait a minute. I just *dreamed* about being

on that flight when all the terrible stuff happened and we were kidnapped . . . *and it felt all too real. As real as this, anyway.*

A round flash of light struck the lawn from the sky. I backed away from the window slowly, panic building by the second.

"What's going on here?"

Another beam of light struck the lawn, moving in an arc, like a searchlight.

Then I saw the tip of a large, dark boomerang pass over the house. *The boomerang craft from my dream.*

I stumbled backward, tripping over the chair in a fluster. My head filled with a sick daze, a sort of white noise, or static. I felt on the verge of throwing up.

A green flashing light strobed on the lawn.

"Oh, no. Please. This can't be happening!" My whole body trembled.

I bolted to the bedroom door and charged down the hallway towards Kelly's room, my heart hammering, my legs growing weaker with each stride.

"Kelly. Not Kelly. Not again," I cried. Tears streamed down my face. Everything seemed *wrong. Like in a dream.* I couldn't be sure of anything. Nothing felt real. I couldn't even feel the floor beneath me. I felt weightless.

A bright light shone from beneath Kelly's door. I could see the shadows of figures through the crack at the bottom.

A strange hum filled my ears.

I grabbed the door knob, hot to the touch, and threw the door open!

I cried out, falling against the door frame, slumping to the floor, washed in a bright white light.

My eyes adjusted quickly to the glare.

Through Kelly's opened bedroom window, I saw the boomerang craft hovering over the yard outside, just over the treetops.

Then I saw her.

Kelly floated above her bed, her eyes wide with terror, her body rigid.

Four black blobs of water bobbed in the air around her, bathed in the white light.

I watched from the door in horror as one poured a small drop of itself into each of her eyes!

With a horrified cry, my trembling hands reached out to stop them.

15

The blue light in the alien's eyes faded to white, then to black. The static filling my head cleared, leaving a splitting headache in its wake.

I felt a drop of blood run from my nose.

The strobing red light above me and the flurry of activity brought me fully back to the control room aboard the alien craft, and the grim situation I faced.

"NO! I'm here. No, I don't want to be here. Why? I don't understand. My house. Kelly's room. Did that really happen?" I asked the grey figure standing in front of me.

"Yes." The voice screeched inside a burst of static in my head.

I couldn't believe it. I shook my head and closed my eyes for a moment thinking I imagined the voice. No. It had to be my friend!

Did he talk to me, through the static?

"Yes." the voice answered in response. It was barely a whisper and hard to understand, but in my head nonetheless. My heart pounded with excitement. *He could speak to me!*

I had a million questions. Who were they? What were they doing here? What did they want? All of those questions, and more, flew from my mind as quickly as they had come, replaced with something more relevant to the current grim situation.

I looked past my new friend to the vast storeroom, filled with hundreds of the frozen, black, waterblobs. The same creatures that attacked Kelly in the dream. The same creature that Kelly herself had become.

"They did this to her, not you. Right?" I asked.

The creature seemed to concentrate. His eyes narrowed and he grimaced. A burst of static filled my head again along with the faint voice. "Not only Kelly."

My stomach hollowed. I swallowed hard as I peered from canister to canister.

Could it be people in those canisters? People like Kelly, implanted and turned into one of those parasitic things? Or were they simply alien prisoners of war?

"They…were once human,…like your sister. Too late for them…" The alien passed his hand sadly in front of the glass. "They…are now of the Cepheid. No longer…human. No identity. No…memories…"

My heart sank. All those people used to have lives of their own with children and families. No one knows what happened to them. No one would ever find them.

Then the thought of what would happen if all those things got loose sent shivers of horror down my spine.

I saw what *one* could do.

"The Cepheid. Are those the waterblobs that attacked Kelly in her room? The things flying that boomerang ship?"

The alien nodded. He seemed tired and reluctant to speak. The mind-to-mind communication, however he did it, must have sapped all his strength.

I had a million more questions about the Cepheid but he couldn't answer, I could tell. I settled for one.

"You said it was too late for them," I choked out, pointing to the rows and rows of frosty canisters behind the glass wall. A lump swelled in my throat.

"Is it too late for Kelly?"

He looked at me with sorrowful eyes. I felt my heart turn to stone, preparing to hear the words I didn't want to hear.

Suddenly, a clatter rose behind us.

I turned in time to hear the growing roar of something sliding up the elevator shaft at great speed. Of something cracking and shattering.

WITH AN EXPLOSIVE CRASH, the elevator car smashed *up* and *out* of the elevator shaft! Its mangled remains landed in a smoking, twisted wad on the floor in front of us.

Something threw it up the shaft, following close behind.

"IT'S KELLY! SHE'S ALIVE!" I cried.

A large black wave of water plunged out of the shaft and into the room. A dozen streams of thin, green beams fired from the aliens' weapons.

The beams flew everywhere as they bounced off the Cepheid, which was re-forming in the middle of the control room.

My alien friend grabbed me and ran through a hidden door in the glass wall, leading to the room full of Cepheid-filled canisters.

I could hear the shouts and cries of the grey aliens behind me as we ran between the rows of canisters. I could see the reflections of their lasers on the glass wall as we ran.

A panel slid open on the far end of the storeroom. *An exit!*

"WAIT! STOP! That's KELLY back there! WE HAVE TO STOP!"

A loud explosion boomed from the control room and all the canisters began to tilt in their stands, a creeping white fog hissing from the tops and bottoms.

The alien stopped running, a horrified look sweeping his pale face.

"Oh, man. They're defrosting! RUN! RUN FOR IT!" I cried, grabbing the alien's hand and hauling him toward the exit.

Black water began to drip onto the white tile floor from the bottoms of hundreds and hundreds of canisters.

16

The panel slid shut behind us and I found myself in a circular hallway like the one I had been *hovered* down before, in the medical chair.

The stars shone brightly outside, ten times brighter than they looked from Earth. They almost hurt to look at. If I had the time, I could have picked out every constellation because I knew each of them by heart. I wondered if I would ever see them from my backyard lawn chair again, like I had so many summers in the past.

The alien ran down the hall, and I followed. From behind, they looked almost human. Smaller and muscular, with grey skin, but their motions and actions seemed very human.

And they definitely had *feelings*.

I had watched this creature display

emotions that looked like fear, sadness, regret, understanding, concern and anger, just about everything. He even stood up for me with the other aliens, talking them into letting me into that control room instead of just letting Kelly catch me.

He displayed many human-like emotions, everything except happiness. I couldn't help but wonder if they were capable of that as well.

He ducked over to a door panel, much like the closet Kelly and I hid in.

"They're coming, you know! Hundreds of them! That Cepheid-Kelly thing managed to let them go! We're as good as dead," I cried.

He pressed his hand into a locking mechanism and it drifted open, a bank of overhead lights springing on in the room.

A medical lab.

A small table sat in the middle of the room with a large, white plastic machine that looked like an upturned chandelier hanging over it, poking into a hole in the ceiling.

A thin sheet of pale rubber covered a rack which looked like it could lower to cover the table. A grid or diagram of some type marked the table which glowed with a pale green light.

Storage panels and crates, like the ones I saw in the storage closet, sat against the walls.

The alien darted behind a thin metal screen that split the wedge-shaped room in two. A soft, machine-like whine whirring to life on the other side.

I carefully walked over and peeked around . . .

Gasping as I saw rows and rows of hover-chairs, like the ones we had been carted around in, all backed into sockets in the wall, the arms from each chair extended and plugged into the wall above it.

"What are you doing? We have to get out of here before she finds us!" I noticed hundreds of small rectangular cartridges plugged into the wall opposite the chairs and a grid-covered table in front of them.

The alien turned around furiously and shoved me back around the screen as if angered, chattering loudly in a parental tone.

"What!? What did I do?"

A long, loud screech answered my question, along with another shove.

"All right! All right! I'll wait out here!"

I rolled my shoulder to adjust my shirt,

and walked closer to the table.

Those things had thawed out by now, probably flying all around the ship . . . and that Cepheid-Kelly thing would come looking for me.

Well, if my alien friend wouldn't do anything, *I would.*

I looked around for something to bar the door, something to stop the things from coming in. But what? Crates? That wouldn't seal the door. Could the door panel be water-tight already?

Then my eyes widened, my legs started knocking, my breathing shallowed, and my heart thumped loudly in my chest.

The door to the med lab sighed . . .

And began to slide open.

17

It floated into the room, the sound of rushing water following its every move.

The sounds of weapons firing and alien screeching stopped as the door slid shut behind the Cepheid.

It had to be Kelly.

It turned and shifted in the air, as if looking for something or someone.

That someone being me.

I kept quiet, hunkered down into a cabinet that I pried open and slipped inside. I kept my eyes locked on it through a narrow crack in the panel.

The black ball of water rippled and shook in the air, the bright lights overhead reflecting off its surface like sunlight on a lake. It would drift one way and then the other, as if on an invisible track.

It seemed to know I was in here; it just didn't know where.

My legs cramped and ached. As small as I am, the compartment seemed even smaller. I didn't move. I didn't breathe. I knew the slightest movement would send the door to the cabinet flying open, leaving me exposed, sitting on a shelf.

A shark! I got the idea that maybe it sensed changes in air currents, like a shark does in water. The slightest movement from me would stir the air, striking its surface, letting it know exactly where I was.

It floated directly in front of me now.

It shifted in the air like a blob of mercury, flowing into itself, heading toward the cabinet.

I swallowed a terrified yell as I heard a *waterfall* inches from the cabinet door.

I held my breath, drawing together as tightly as I could.

Motionless.

The light dimmed as it approached the narrow gap I left in the panel door. The light that filtered through rippled on my face.

I almost gasped as a small seam of water

filled the crack of the cabinet . . .

And pulled away, drifting toward the metal screen splitting the room.

NO! *My friend. He's as good as dead.*

Then I saw him, the grey alien, carefully easing around the screen as the waterblob started around the opposite end.

I wanted to signal him. To warn him. But I couldn't. It would find me.

Still. He helped me. Saved my life more than once. I owed him, didn't I?

I braced myself, preparing to jump out of the cabinet and draw its attention, ready to run like crazy for my life.

Before I could do *anything,* the alien pulled out a boxy device, aiming it at my cabinet!

The cabinet door suddenly slid open!

I was left uncovered! Unbalanced!

I fell out, yelling and crying!

"NO! KELLY! NO!"

The waterblob roared, the voice inside it shrieking, racing toward me, ballooning out into a large watery umbrella!

For an instant I watched black doom unfold over my head.

"NO!" I shouted, *rolling to the side,*

sensing a flash of light and searing blast of cold.

WHAM! A frozen, black ball of ice slammed into the floor beside me, then bounced once . . . twice . . . and rolled to a frosty, smoking stop against the table.

18

I lay there for a moment, staring at the smoking ball of ice, *my sister.*

Past the table stood my friend, a larger boxy weapon in his hands, still aimed at the black ball of ice.

Two other greys rushed into the room, chattering wildly with my friend as they saw the frozen Cepheid and me.

I just lay still on the floor, staring at Kelly . . . until the grey aliens picked up the ball of ice with gloved hands.

"NO! Leave her alone! Can't you just leave her alone? Let us go. Let us both go." I started crying, sobbing in great gasps. I knew it was too late. The look on their faces said it all.

They solemnly took the ball of ice behind the screen to the table. I jumped up, running to join her, but was stopped abruptly by two grey arms.

The static filled my head, making me wince in pain. My teeth ached, and my head felt like it would split. My friend leaned into my face, a sorrowful look in his eyes.

"Morgan ... you must ... trust me. I wil try and ... help your sister ... but you ... must trust me."

I nodded, tears in my eyes. Struggling weakly and in vain against him. He hadn't betrayed my trust so far and I could think of no other option.

I could hear the other two aliens in my mind, through the static.

"I have found her file. Loading now."

"He shouldn't see this, Krel."

Krell. His name is Krell. All this time. All we had been through and he never told me his name.

The other two came out from behind the screen, as my friend Krell stepped away.

They held me closely, turning my head away from the screen.

The lights dimmed in the room.

I heard a loud whirring sound and a series of clicks, like something locking into place.

Suddenly a burst of blinding light filled the room, followed by a tortured scream! A SCREAM OF INCREDIBLE PAIN! *A human, female scream.*

I tried to turn and look, to see what he was doing to Kelly, but the two others held my head, not allowing me to see.

The light intensified.

I wanted to run behind the screen and stop him.

The screaming grew louder.

Then the lights dimmed to normal. Their grips loosened as they stepped away.

I turned to see my alien friend Krell walk from behind the screen.

I wanted to ask, but couldn't. The words choked in my throat and I could see the answer in his solemn face.

"No."

A smile, a faint smile crept across his mouth, his dark eyes lit up from behind.

Kelly ran from behind the screen!

They did it! They saved her!

She ran straight to me and we hugged, clutching at each other.

A flood of joy filled me, making me forget

everything else.

"I can't believe it! You're alive! And you're *you!*" I touched her head, her hair to be sure.

She wore a silver smock, like in a hospital, and slippers, the material unlike any I had ever seen. Her arms shook and she seemed weak.

She looked around, trembling and shaking, terrified of the grey aliens.

"It's okay, Kelly. They're all right. They're trying to help us. Help *all* of us."

Kelly didn't seem to believe me, but didn't panic. She clung to my arm, trying not to fall over.

"Wha . . . What's going on, Morgan? The last thing I remember was seeing *him* on the plane!" she exclaimed, pointing at Krell. Her legs seemed weak and she couldn't keep her balance. Her arms and legs flopped limply as I struggled to hold her up.

Krell motioned for us to follow him, as the other two grey aliens opened the door and stepped into the hall, weapons drawn.

"We're in a serious situation, Kelly. I'll explain later."

I hugged her hard again, just to be sure I wasn't dreaming *this* time. She struggled to her feet and held her head, wincing.

"C'mon. We'll get home. Just trust me."

We stepped out into the hall.

A strange beep sounded loudly, like a fire alarm or something.

The aliens shrieked, dropping their weapons as Kelly and I screamed.

There, outside the windows in the hall-way, blocking the stars from the sky, hovered *a boomerang-shaped craft, its bright white search-lights sweeping through the windows.*

19

"It's them!" I yelled.

"Who are they?" Kelly cried, watching the searing white light sweeping down the hall toward us. She looked at me with terror-filled eyes.

I saw her in my mind, floating two feet over her bed, the waterblobs hovering all around her in the bright-white light, their boomerang craft rotating over our house in Fairfield.

"You've met them before, *in your room,* you just don't remember! RUN! RUN! HURRY!"

The beam swept the hallway behind us as we ran; Kelly, myself, Krell, and the other two grey aliens.

I kept glancing to the side, out the windows, hoping to see the end of the boomerang craft as it gently drifted up and down. Its dark surface suddenly lit up with small red lights.

Then I saw the bodies.

Grey-black alien bodies littered the hallway as we approached a twisted hole in the wall, a smashed elevator door panel lying against the wall opposite it.

The bodies lay face down, absolutely drenched, puddles of black water forming beneath them.

Kelly froze upon seeing them, gasping for breath, clutching her stomach. Her eyes glazed over with wild fear.

"Oh, no. Not again. It's THEM! IN MY ROOM! THEY'VE TRAPPED ME! THEY'RE HURTING ME!"

She was remembering.

"Don't look, Kelly. Just run past them, quick!" I grabbed her arm and pulled, trying to follow Krell and the others into the elevator shaft.

Kelly shook and screamed, her eyes locked onto the bodies, watching the puddles dripping *up* into their eyes and mouths.

"*ME!* That's what happened to *me!* They did that to me! They were in my . . . my room . . . *MY* room and they did that to me! They went . . . into my *eyes!*" Kelly started to cry and shake, stumbling to the ground beside the doomed grey alien.

I pulled at her, tugging and yanking her along. "Don't do this to me! NOT NOW! We have to gooooo!"

A white beam of light froze our crouched bodies in the hall.

The boomerang found us.

A pale green beam struck us through the window, like a million needles stabbing my brain.

I saw Krell rush from the elevator shaft, shrieking loudly, his friends trying to stop him.

I fell over, and so did Kelly.

I watched Kelly's head drop onto the back of the doomed alien which had stopped her, the water puddles beneath them pulling away.

As my head hit the floor, I felt a warm wetness on my cheek.

Then the darkness fell.

20

My eyes opened suddenly, peering through the darkness of the room.

Kelly rolled over, asleep in bed, her pajama leg hiked up over her shin, the sheets crumpled around her. Her snoring was muffled by the pillow flopped on her head.

I rubbed my eyes, rising on unsteady legs in the doorway to her bedroom.

How did I get there?

Sleepwalking. How weird. I never did that before. I felt disoriented, fuzzy. I turned and shuffled down the hall toward my room.

The hallway faded . . . and I found myself being carried, looking down from a high catwalk to a dark control room, small grey figures shooting at and fleeing from hundreds of black blobs whizzing through the air around them.

"WHOA!" I could hardly breathe, waves of panic flowing through me. *Did that just happen? Am I still asleep?* The wall of the upstairs hall felt comforting against my hand.

I staggered through the doorway to my room. My computer monitor glowed from the corner, the modem lights blinking on and off rapidly receiving a signal.

The television flickered, static filling the screen.

I could have sworn I turned it off.

The static from the television grew louder, in my head now, giving me a tremendous headache. I clapped my hands to my ears, wincing in pain.

I saw a bright, white light sweeping through my backyard.

A voice in my head, barely audible, broke through the static.

"We help as much ... as we can ... homes ... no longer safe ... come at night ... thousands and thousands ... some of your people know ... but ignore the obvious ... hide the truth ... hope ..."

A blinding pain shot through my head.

"Don't let .... the same thing ... happen to your world ... that happened to ours."

"Krell. KRELL! is that you?" I could barely understand the voice through the pain.

"Be aware..."

The light came through the window.

There were too many stars outside my bedroom window and they seemed too bright.

A white light engulfed me, flooding the room.

"NOOOO!" My hands shot up, trying to stop them, though I knew it was futile.

One by one, I watched the Cepheid float in through my bedroom window; black blobs of water rippling and drifting through the air, roaring like waterfalls.

They surrounded me as their boomerang craft hovered outside over the yard, slowly rotating in the air.

I couldn't move, couldn't fight.

I felt myself begin to float up from the floor, paralyzed!

Everything grew dark as they spread over me.

I heard a deafening rush of water as I felt the first drops . . .

21

I woke up on a smooth metal floor, bathed in a bright blue light.

A pair of large black eyes stared down at me from a small grey alien.

"Uhh, where am I?" I sat up abruptly with a loud humming in my head, hoping that this was all still a dream.

No such luck.

One of Krell's friends stared at me, from a low, armless chair, molded from the same metal as the floor.

Low, dark archways circled the dome-shaped room, from ceiling to floor.

The floor vibrated with a strange noise, unlike any I had heard before, like a high-energy crackle.

A small dome, the size of a basketball, sat

in the middle of the room on the floor. A large rounded pipe ran from the dome to the ceiling, where it vanished into a complex array of machinery.

It looked very close to the books and reports I read; the disks at Nellis Air Force Base, the Roswell, New Mexico incident.

I was in a flying saucer.

I stood, half-expecting to fall over, ready to balance myself because of the great speed we were probably traveling.

Nothing. No sense of speed at all.

"Are we moving?" I asked as the alien moved to my side, helping me up.

He nodded and pointed past the chairs, past the dome, to a bank of low control panels and the alien piloting the craft.

"KRELL!"

My friend turned and nodded. In front of him, the sloped wall blinked, faded and became *transparent.*

An *ocean* of rushing pine trees came into view, low lying mountains passing at incredible speed below us.

"Oh, man. We're back home. You brought us back. KELLY! Where's Kelly?"

I heard a groan in response as my sister rose from the floor on the other side of the saucer.

"Kelly! Are you all right?"

"I think so. Where . . . never mind. I don't want to know," she moaned, clutching her head.

"They're taking us home, Kelly. Home!"

I rushed to help her up, a smile spreading across my face.

"The image I saw when I passed out. The control room! Hundreds of black blobs fighting the greys. It must have *not* been a dream. We escaped! Krell and his friends got us out of there!"

The saucer suddenly lurched to the left, as the aliens chattered loudly!

The wall in front of me blinked and faded, bubbling and warping right in front of my eyes.

Half the floor beneath me *vanished, leaving me suspended in midair.*

I cried out, grasping for Kelly's hand.

22

I stared down, my heart in my throat, watching the tops of the trees flying past beneath my sneakers.

Kelly grabbed my hand, clinging to an archway which also began to fade.

A strange blue-white glow warped along the floor and across the wall with a crackling sound.

I wasn't falling.

Then I realized that as the glow passed through them, the floors and walls had turned transparent.

"It's a gravity field, Kelly! It moves the ship along, just like in the books, and like I saw from the plane!"

"W-what are you talking about?" Kelly stammered.

I watched it a moment more. Entire sections of the saucer became transparent as the field passed through it, distorting it as if I were looking through a thick glass.

"It's all true! Don't you get it? All the stories about crashed disks, abductions, element 115. It's all true! We're seeing it all first-hand!"

Krell chattered to his friend loudly and with alarm, but I couldn't tear my eyes away from the incredible sight of the passing energy field.

I watched with wonderment as the gravity wave sped along the wall, fading it as it went, revealing clouds, stars and . . .

The boomerang craft following close behind!

"NO!" My heart sank. My stomach knotted as a cry of disbelief left my mouth.

"They found us! KRELL! THEY FOUND US!"

Kelly and I ran to the front of the saucer, nearly knocking my alien friend out of his seat.

"Do something! Quick!" I yelled.

Krell pressed a series of pads on his control console and the front wall vanished. We saw the edge of a mountain pass beneath us, hundreds of feet to the valley floor below.

"Wait! NO!" Kelly cried.

We gasped as Krell took the saucer straight down at an incredible speed.

The saucer skirted the tops of the trees, skiing down a long row of power lines that led to the bottom of the mountain.

"SLOW DOWN! MORGAN! TELL HIM TO SLOW DOWN!" Kelly yelled.

A lake came into view at the bottom of the mountain, approaching fast.

"Uh, Morgan?" Kelly asked, her eyes growing wide with terror.

"Up! Up now! Krell! TAKE IT UP! NOW! OH, NOOOOOO!" I cried.

We skimmed the surface of the lake at rocket speed. It had to be Lake Wataga! I could see the Hungry Bear restaurant and the lights of the cabins on the shore.

A large, brown hump rose in the middle of the lake, but vanished with a huge splash as we soared past.

"Morgan, what was that?"

"I have no idea. LOOK OUT!"

The boomerang craft sped past us to the left, circling around to the front, CUTTING US OFF!

Krell grimaced and took the saucer straight up.

The craft fired a bolt of green light, missing us, but striking the lake.

We flew up and out . . . over the forest at an incredible speed, the blur of green below us turning brown.

In a flash we had reached Lost Cove National Park, *seventy five miles* away from Lake Wataga.

Krell's friend touched a control pad on the console in front of him. Dozens of voices, human voices, started squawking in garbled tones through walls of static, like a bad radio, all talking about an unknown object in the skies over three counties . . . so far. A UFO!

"US! They're talking about us! They have us on radar!"

"Morgan, look!" Kelly grabbed my head and made me look straight down.

Through the transparent floor, I saw the boomerang craft flying straight up at us, rotating onto its back in the air.

All three search lights moved into a triangle formation, snapping straight up . . .

Locked in and ready to fire.

23

A searing green blast rocked the saucer from below.

"WE'VE BEEN HIT!" I yelled as Kelly grabbed the console.

For a moment, the saucer spun powerless, hanging in the air.

Then we plunged.

I closed my eyes as we fell, the sensation of falling freezing my brain with absolute terror.

My worst fear came to life.

I felt myself plunging, faster and faster, no hope for rescue, only the immovable ground rushing up to meet me, eager to break my fall.

I could feel the impact in my mind, hear my terrified scream cut short by a sudden, echoing burst.

SUDDENLY, a tremendous surge, *a giant*

blue-white wave, erupted from the dome in the center of the room.

Krell regained control.

The entire craft turned transparent!

I drifted from the archway, a cry swelling in my throat, the sight of the open sky startling me.

I felt weightless, suspended in mid-air, my arms and legs spreading out in shock.

For an instant . . . I felt a strange exhilaration, almost a joy.

The sensation of free flight!

For the first time, height, speed, and the sensation of falling didn't bother me.

For that instant, I couldn't see or think of anything else. Not the aliens, not the saucer, not the attacking craft . . . only the wonderful sensation of flight.

Something I had never felt before.

In a flash, the surge subsided and gravity returned, sending us all to the floor.

Krell guided the saucer into the valley below, the boomerang craft close behind. His friend sat down, chattering loudly, helping him with the guidance controls.

"NO! They're still behind us! We have to outrun them! They're gaining!" Kelly stared out of the back of the saucer at the sinister lights of the boomerang craft, gliding behind us like a shark, approaching fast.

The steep gorges of Lost Cove National Park rose all around, trees and shrubs sliced through by the crackling energy surrounding the saucer.

Through the bottom of the craft, I could see tall trees doubling over, crushed under the white-blue energy field.

I turned to Krell as he banked the saucer hard around a tree-covered hill, sending a herd of deer running for their lives.

I swallowed hard, afraid of the answer before I asked. "If they hit us again, we're dead. Right?"

Krell nodded.

I looked behind me, a sickening dread growing in my stomach.

Kelly crouched in front of the transparent back wall, giving scale to the massive dark craft following close behind.

Gaining steadily.

"Krell, there has to be something we can do." I felt my breath shallowing, my stomach flooding with dread.

They were going to catch us. Nothing could prevent that. At the rate they were gaining, we had only moments left to live.

Krell looked over at us solemnly, his hands slipping from the panels.

He reached down and pressed a very small panel on the side of the console . . .

Sliding it open.

An orange glow lit the inside of the compartment.

I couldn't believe it.

"Is that what I think it is?" I asked.

24

A small triangular piece of orange metal sat inside the compartment.

It slowly slid out on a tray, the orange glow lighting my face like a miniature sun.

"Element 115."

Krell nodded.

The super-dense element glowed and sparkled in front of me. I once read it could create a gravity wave completely out of synch with the natural gravity around it. I never thought it could really *exist*.

"What does this mean? What are . . . wait a minute." With shock, I looked up at Krell, whose face also reflected the element's brilliant glow.

I remembered reading in one of my books about an accident rumored to have happened with element 115 at Groom Lake.

Something went wrong in a craft the Air Force scientists were test-piloting, one they had built using alien technology. Something about the power source. It exploded with the force of a small nuclear bomb.

I swallowed hard.

"What are you going to do?" I asked.

"They're firing! THEY'RE FIRING!" Kelly screamed, pointing at the craft roaring up behind, *only yards from the saucer.*

Krell frantically ran his hands over the console, a loud hum building in the dome toward the center of the room.

The boomerang lunged forward like a charging bull! A fiery energy field surrounded it like green lightning, gathering on the nose in a crackling, white ball.

"LOOK OUT!" I cried.

A bolt of the green energy field leapt off the front of the boomerang and blasted straight toward us!

Kelly and I screamed as the saucer flew straight up, narrowly dodging the beam that flew toward a grove of trees below.

A tremendous explosion shattered the

forest as it struck.

The saucer rolled and straightened, heading straight toward the boomerang craft!

"WAIT! WE'RE HEADING RIGHT FOR THEM! STOP!" Kelly cried out.

The boomerang banked away sharply, narrowly avoiding a fence-lined hill. The lights from its underside swept over the grass like searchlights.

We sailed past them as they shot away, the tops of the trees vanishing below us, fading into a starry sky.

"YES! ALL RIGHT! We missed them!"

The saucer banked left and down, lurching forward, rushing straight for the boomerang!

We were chasing them!

"HEY!" I yelled.

"WHAT ARE YOU DOING? ARE YOU CRAZY? MORGAN, STOP HIM!" Kelly yelled, clutching an archway as the saucer shook violently.

Krell's face wrinkled and his eyes narrowed. His hands moved quickly over the console. He turned to look at me, his eyes lit up with a faint blue glow.

I heard the familiar static in my head, felt

the headache start, a faint voice echoing through the pain.

"I didn't understand. Say it again!" I watched the boomerang skim along the walls of the gorge as we gained speed, closing in fast.

My heart leaped from my chest and my face flushed with nervous excitement.

Krell repeated himself in my mind.

I shot a glance over to him in disbelief.

"I don't think that's such a good idea."

A green stream of lightning jumped from
the edge of the saucer, snaking through the air,
striking the boomerang craft.

The energy stream held the sinister ship
in place, like a lasso of energy.

Both crafts slowed to a stop over a deep,
tree-covered valley, pulling and tugging each
other as if tied together with a chain.

"This is too dangerous!" I yelled.

*The grey aliens stopped the boomerang in
midair, the same as they had done with the
plane.*

Kelly hunched down on the floor, never
taking her eyes off the boomerang tumbling and
rolling in the air before us. The Cepheid's ship.

"They're on there. Those black water
things. THEY'RE GOING TO GET LOOSE AND

THEY'RE GOING TO COME AFTER US!" She was trembling and her voice sounded frantic, terrified.

I watched the boomerang craft through the transparent wall of the saucer. It jerked and rotated, trying to break free, knocking down trees and gouging the side of a rocky cliff as it turned.

The lasso of lightning held firm.

Krell's friend chattered loudly, yelling and screeching. They argued back and forth.

"WHY ARE WE HOLDING ON TO THAT THING?" Kelly shrieked.

I knew why.

"Kelly, help me!" I cried.

I grabbed the chunk of orange metal as Krell had instructed in my mind, trying to lift it up.

I couldn't even *budge it.*

"Krell! It's too heavy!" I yelled.

He glanced over to me with glowing blue eyes, the green lasso of energy reflecting on his face.

Neither he nor the other grey aliens could leave the control panel.

"Kelly, PLEASE! Help me!" I grunted, pulling and tugging at the chunk of metal.

Though it couldn't have been over two inches long, it weighed at least a hundred pounds.

"What? What are you doing? WHAT IS THAT THING! I'M NOT TOUCHING IT!"

"PLEASE! Help me take it to the reaction chamber."

"The what?"

"The dome in the middle of the room! Quick! We have to hurry!"

Together we pulled the metal off the tray. We struggled, barely able to carry it toward the dome, the hum growing louder as we approached.

The dome lifted from the floor, pulled by a control rod that ran into the complex machinery above.

Beneath the rising dome, a small triangular chunk of metal rested in a metal bowl surrounded by bizarre machinery.

I could hear the whirring and crackling of electrical energy as we approached the complex array surrounding the glowing metal, the power source of the ship.

Strange, blue flashes of light leapt from the bowl in bursts, sweeping into us.

The bursts knocked us back, like powerful ocean waves. They surged over my arms and legs, pushing against me. A feeling of sea sickness rocked my body with each burst.

"QUICK! We have to put the metal in the bowl," I yelled over the hum.

"There's already a chunk there! What will happen?" Kelly yelled back.

I turned to look at Krell who looked back, his eyes still glowing blue.

"You don't want to know."

"Great."

"On THREE! Ready? One . . . two . . ."

"WAIT! Toss it ON three or right after three?" Kelly asked.

"ON THREE! READY?"

Krell and the other alien ran to a small octagonal panel concealed in the floor near the wall toward the front.

They both disappeared.

"Where did they go? They didn't ditch us, did they?" Kelly yelled craning her neck, her eyes wide in fear.

I turned to Kelly, matching her terrified expression with my own.

The same thought crossed my mind as I felt the growing weight in my hand begin to slip.

Then Krell spoke in my head, reassuring

me of their intentions.

"Trust them!" I yelled. "READY?"

"ONE . . ."

The boomerang craft rotated swiftly around, the triangular pattern of lights sweeping through the sky.

"TWO . . ."

We hoisted the metal up to the bowl in a swinging motion.

Krell popped out of the hatch, scrambling to the control console.

"THREE . . ."

The metal slammed into the bowl, striking the other metal chunk with a loud CLANG as the dome lowered.

"C'MON! HURRY!" I yelled.

Kelly and I scrambled across the floor to the control consoles at the front of the saucer. The waves from the erupting dome pounded our backs, knocking us off balance.

Krell quickly grabbed us and pushed us over the control console.

We fell through an open hatch on the other side, another alien pulling us through the opening.

We fell a few feet and landed on the floor

of a small, acorn-shaped room, about ten feet in diameter, blue-white light shining from all directions.

Krell and his friend landed hard, right beside us.

I felt a sudden heart-stopping plunge.

Through the transparent roof of the acorn, I watched the bottom of the saucer speeding up and away! We had to be in an escape pod!

Falling . . .

At an enormous rate of speed . . .

Pine tree branches snapped and broke as they hurtled past, partially obscuring our view of the two ships locked together in the starry night sky.

Two alien hands grabbed our heads, hiding our eyes as a bone-crushing EXPLOSION rocked the acorn-shaped escape pod, *sending it tumbling end-over-end.*

Our eyes burned and stung with a tremendous blast of heat and light.

Our screams were swallowed up by an explosive sound a million times greater than the loudest Fourth of July.

The ground thudded beneath us, and with a sudden jerk . . .

It ended.

The four of us stood and peered at the sight: a charred patch of ground, flattened trees, scorched earth about the length of a football field.

No wreckage. No debris. Nothing.

Complete annihilation.

The night air, cool and dry, kissed our cheeks like a welcome home.

The small metal acorn, with an open hatch on the side, sat on the ground beneath a splintered tree.

Inside, a beacon strobed like crazy, beaming co-ordinates at an undetectable frequency.

"Kelly, we're home." I said, a wide grin spreading across my face.

"WE'RE HOME!" Kelly and I shouted together with joy, hugging each other tight.

Beneath the stars at the bottom of a valley, a brother and sister from the neighborhood and two friends from out-of-town hugged and laughed.

They shared a brief moment of union and victory.

27

From an old wooden chair in front of my jumbled desk, I watched the modem lights blink. I kicked back and spun around with my arms folded behind my head.

It would take only a few moments more for my story to upload to MUFON (the Mutual UFO Network), an international organization studying the UFO phenomenon.

I'm sure they'll take my story more seriously than the *other* investigators did.

And *that* was weeks ago.

Flight 341 landed without further incident and only five minutes behind schedule. The crew and the passengers were unable to account for the massive blackout and unable to remember anything that happened *during* the blackout. Dad read in the paper that Air Force investigators were being called in but they would never say why.

Kelly and I knew why.

Our *friends* dropped us off in Potter's field, about two miles away from our house.

We stood in the field and watched the rescue saucer slowly rise into the sky, the bright rings of blue and red circling around the rim. A bright beam of light washed over us in a flash, then again.

A goodbye, I supposed.

We smiled and waved as the saucer rose faster and faster, the blue-white glow beneath shining as bright as a star.

"Thanks, Krell," I said softly as the saucer became another star in the sky, and then . . .

A memory.

We showed up on our doorstep four hours late and reported missing from the flight.

Of course, no one really believed our story, not even Mom and Dad, though no one has come up with a better explanation yet.

Kelly poked her head around my bedroom door, her perfect hair pulled back in a pony-tail, a broad smile on her face, a pile of books and CD-ROMs in her hands.

"Morgan, I'm going to drop all this stuff off at the library. Did we need anything else?"

I handed her a list of books. More research on UFO's to do, *together*.

"These will do . . . for now."

"Hi, Morgan!" a sweet voice called from behind Kelly.

"Hi, Shelly."

Shelly Miller. One of Kelly's friends. Real strong. Real cute, but a little bossy. She hangs around with my friend Curtis a lot.

Kelly eyed the list and smiled. "No problem. Listen, you want to go? Shelly and I will probably go to the mall afterward."

"I don't know," I grinned.

"C'mon. It'll be fun. Shelly wants to tell you something *weird* that happened to her and Curtis," Kelly begged.

"PLEASE? It's important. I'll buy the pizza." When Shelly asked, it was more of a demand . . . *and* she could kick my butt.

I turned the monitor off.

"Okay, but this story better be a good one." I stood up and started toward the door.

"Oh, it is," Shelly called, disappearing down the hall.

"Just give me a minute," I said, closing the door behind them.

Kelly sure treats me different now. We do everything together and we get along great. (She even drags me away from the computer to meet her new friends! Something she *never* did before.)

I walked over to my open window and looked out at the night sky. A million stars twinkled above me. *A shooting star cut across my field of vision, fading in the blink of an eye.*

What a beautiful night.

I saw an image of the shining saucer over Potter's field in my mind and couldn't help but wonder.

Would I ever see Krell again?

A static suddenly filled my head.

A searing pain swelled behind my eyes, filling my ears, knocking me off balance. I stumbled over my chair and fell to the floor.

I could hear a faint voice in my head, through the static and the pain, barely audible, almost a whisper.

"Morgan...hang ...on! ...On our ...way!"

"KRELL!" I cried.

My nose began to bleed, as it always did when he talked to me through my mind. I felt weak, sick. A chill swept through my body.

"What's happening? Why are you coming back?" I shouted.

Kelly opened the door to my room and shrieked as she saw me, the sight sending her reeling back.

A drop ran from my nose and splattered the back of my hand.

I looked down and froze in horror.

Not blood . . .

Black water,

About the Authors

Marty M. Engle and **Johnny Ray Barnes Jr.**, graduates of the Art Institute of Atlanta, are the creators, writers, designers and illustrators of the **Strange Matter™** series and the **Strange Matter™** World Wide Web page.

Their interests and expertise range from state of the art 3-D computer graphics and interactive multi-media, to books and scripts (television and motion picture).

Marty lives in La Jolla, California with his wife Jana and twin terror pets, Polly and Oreo.

Johnny Ray lives in Tierrasanta, California and spends every free moment with his fiancée, Meredith.

And now an exciting preview of the next

#8 Frozen Dinners

by Johnny Ray Barnes, Jr.

1

"See anything out there, Max?" Uncle Shoe asked.

As I looked out the window at the forest which surrounded my uncle's mountain home, I noticed it was the first morning since we'd arrived that everything wasn't covered in fog.

"It's so clear outside. I can see everything," I said, my breath clouding the window.

Uncle Shoe's two story home stood on one of the highest levels of the mountain, with no neighbors in sight. He was sort of a hermit, and liked to keep things simple. Fireplaces for heat, gas lamps for light, and a good book for entertainment. Modern conveniences were of no use to him, except a radio for weather forecasts and a fridge that he powered with a small generator. Otherwise, it looked like he lived in the 19th century.

"You timed your vacation just right." Uncle

Shoe stood up from his chair and lit his pipe. I heard him chuckle a little as he walked up behind me. "It's always this still before a little snow falls. You'll get in some sledding this week after all."

"Snow? Well, that blasts our hiking trip tomorrow," my older brother Mark whined. He sat on the floor, with my uncle's old radio torn into a thousand parts and scattered across an old blanket. It had died just a couple of days before Mark, my sister Teresa, and I came to stay with Uncle Shoe. My brother's an electronic genius, so my uncle left the radio for him to fix.

The visit was my mother's idea. Crier Mountain, where Uncle Shoe lives, is far enough away from Fairfield to make it seem like another world, but still close enough for Mom and Dad to send us there without worrying about us too much. Mom thought it would be nice if we spent a few days of our winter vacation in the mountains. Uncle Shoe doesn't get much company, but he's one of the nicest people I know, and he cares a lot for our whole family.

"The snow'll go soft in a day or so, Mark," said Uncle Shoe. "Plenty of time to walk this mountain. 'Til then you can hit the slopes with Max, or get that old transistor working."

"What about Teresa? Snowy weather could mess up that cel phone signal really nicely," Mark grinned, and pointed a screwdriver over in Teresa's direction.

She hadn't taken her ear from Mom and Dad's cel phone for more than an hour since we'd been at the cabin. Even now she sat crumpled on the couch with her feet in the air, gabbing like she got paid for it.

"Tyler Webb's cute, but he's too young for me. He's Max's age. A sixth grader. Nope, someone like Daniel Meeker, he's for me. And if it snows, I can entertain myself very well, thank you."

I think she and Mark both have screws loose. Why else would they complain about snow? It never piled up as deep in Fairfield as it did in the mountains. We were in the perfect spot to enjoy it.

"Uncle Shoe, seriously, do you think it will snow tonight?" I felt myself shaking a little with excitement. Sure I liked hiking. Sure I liked getting to know nature. And sure I loved listening to Uncle Shoe's stories.

But above all else, I wanted my chance to go sledding.

That's what the snow meant to me.

Shooting down hills at top speed, just on the

ragged edge of losing control of the sled. Isn't that what snow is for?

Uncle Shoe once told me that, when he was a kid, he climbed the mountain just to hit the wildest, roughest slopes around.

That was all I needed to hear.

I'd tamed my skateboard, mastered stump-jumping on my bike. But hard-course sledding was untouched territory for me. Mom always says I'm too much of a daredevil, but if things aren't a little scary, they're just no fun.

"Max," Uncle Shoe said, "I can say with a good amount of certainty that when you wake up tomorrow morning, you will see snow. I feel it in my bones. The question is, what are you going to use to tackle the hills?"

"I've got an inner tube in my suitcase. A big yellow one."

Uncle Shoe's nose crinkled.

"You want to go sledding in a big yellow doughnut? My boy, to go sledding, you need *a sled.*"

Stepping over Mark's wiry mess on the floor, he made his way over to a corner closet. From the way the door popped when he opened it, I thought it'd been glued shut for years. After looking through the stuff inside for a few seconds, Uncle Shoe grabbed for something deep inside.

He pulled out an old wooden sled.

"I call it Thunder Blades. It's yours to use if you can clean it up a bit."

"Sure thing! Thanks!" It looked like a molded piece of wood with two blades like large butter knives attached under it. And it had a lousy name. But I didn't want to hurt Uncle Shoe's feelings. Besides, I'd try anything once.

Then while I was looking it over, I found something.

Scarring the belly of the sled were long, deep cuts in the wood.

I couldn't be sure, but they looked like claw marks.

Introducing

STRANGERS™

An incredible new club exclusively for readers of Strange Matter™

To receive exclusive information on joining this *strange* new organization, simply fill out the slip below and mail to:

STRANGE MATTER INFO •Front Line Art Publishing • 9808 Waples St. • San Diego, California 92121

Name _____ Age _____

Address _____

City _____ State _____ Zip _____

How did you hear about Strange Matter™? _____

_____

What other series do you read? _____

_____

Where did you get this Strange Matter™ book? _____

_____